RUMPLY
STIN

Written by Laurence Anholt
Illustrated by Arthur Robins

ORCHARD BOOKS
96 Leonard Street, London EC2A 4XD
Orchard Books Australia
32/45-51 Huntley Street, Alexandria, NSW 2015
First published in Great Britain in 1996. This edition published in 2002.
Text © Laurence Anholt 1996. Illustrations © Arthur Robins 1996.
The rights of Laurence Anholt to be identified as the author
and Arthur Robins as the illustrator of this work
have been asserted by them in accordance with the
Copyright, Designs and Patents Act, 1988.
A CIP catalogue record for this book is available from the British Library.
ISBN 1 84121 412 4
7 9 10 8 6
Printed in Great Britain

ORCHARD BOOKS

☆ Ghostyshocks ☆ Snow White ☆ Cinderboy ☆ Eco-Wolf ☆
☆ The Greedy Farmer ☆ Billy Beast ☆

There was once a country where everyone had silly names.

They were called 'Mrs Mouse-dropping'
or 'Roland Camelbelly', and they called
their children 'Little Custardlump' or
'Teeny-Tiny Toenail Clipping'.

But the person with the silliest name of all was the king himself and he was very proud of it.

His full title was 'His Royal Niceness Marvin Eggbeard Pyjamadance Birdwhistle Gormangeek Bob-a-job Kneepickle Burp Glub-glub Globba Blobin Eeeeee Woomph Paint-Your-Mother-Green – Junior III'. Which is a pretty good name for a king.

His Royal Niceness
Marvin Eggbeard
Pyjama

Now, in this country lived a miller by the name of Eyebrow Snailsocks. Eyebrow had a beautiful daughter who he was always boasting about, "Not only is she beautiful," he would say, "but she is clever too.

My daughter can do ANYTHING! Why, I bet she could . . . I bet she could . . . make string vests out of spaghetti!"

"Don't be silly, Daddy," the girl would say.
And everyone who knew old Eyebrow
only laughed.

But one day, the king (whose name I have mentioned) heard of Eyebrow's idle boasts.

"Send your daughter to me," he ordered, "let's see how clever she really is."

The miller was very frightened and his daughter began to shake and weep into her apron, but the king's order had to be obeyed.

13

Before she left, Eyebrow promised to buy his daughter anything she wanted to make up for the trouble his boasting had caused.

His daughter couldn't think of anything offhand except perhaps a little fluffy guinea pig for a pet. And this Eyebrow promised her as soon as she returned from the palace. (Assuming she was still wearing her head.)

And so it was that the young girl stood shaking before the king.

"DO YOU KNOW WHO I AM?" he demanded in a deep royal voice.

"Yes sir," whispered the girl. "You are 'His Royal Niceness Marvin Eggbeard Pyjamadance Birdwhistle Gormangeek Bob-a-job Kneepickle Burp Glub-glub Globba Blobin Eeeeee Woomph Paint-Your-Mother-Green – Junior III'."

"Exactly," said the king. "Now, your father has been boasting that you can knit string vests out of spaghetti. I have decided to lock you in a room full of spaghetti and if it isn't all knitted into string vests by sunrise, I will personally tickle your armpits with a wet toothbrush."

Saying this, the king swept out of the
room and went off to practise signing his
name.

The miller's daughter was in despair, she looked at the mountain of spaghetti and thought of the little fluffy guinea pig she would never see. Then she wept into her apron again.

All of a sudden she heard a funny little laugh.

Tee hee hee hee!

And looking down at her feet she saw the strangest little man she had ever seen. He wore a pointy hat and had an orange beard which was so long that he had wrapped it three times around his waist.

"I know," she sobbed. "I have to knit all this spaghetti into string vests otherwise the king will tickle my armpits with a wet toothbrush."

"Oh please help me," sobbed the girl.

The little fellow grabbed an armful of spaghetti and pulled two enormous knitting needles from his pocket. But suddenly, he paused, and looked up at the girl.

The poor girl searched her apron pocket which was soaked with tears and finally pulled out a soggy toffee which the little man seized with delight.

The girl danced with joy as vest after vest
flew from the flashing needles.

Early in the morning the king brought
the miller to watch the toothbrush tickling.

Of course, he couldn't believe his eyes when he unlocked the door and saw that every last bit of spaghetti had been made into perfect little string vests, all with tomato buttons down the front, as neat as you please.

"What did I tell you?" boasted Eyebrow Snailsocks (pretending not to be surprised) "I said she was clever. My daughter can do ANYTHING! Why, I bet . . . I bet she could make bank notes out of OLD FISH."

"Oh Daddy!" groaned the miller's daughter. But it was too late, the king was already ordering a room to be filled to the ceiling with old fish.

"Right!" he shouted. "If she fails I'll . . . let's see . . . I'll plant melon seeds between her toes and . . . if she succeeds then . . . I'll marry her."

Well, the miller's daughter didn't much fancy having melon seeds planted between her toes. . .

. . . but, on the other hand, she didn't like the idea of being married to the king either; especially if she was going to be called 'Her Royal Niceness Marvin Eggbeard Pyjamadance Birdwhistle Gormangeek Bob-a-job etc etc'.

As soon as she was alone with the mountain of fish she began to weep into her apron. Surely no one could make bank notes out of old fish? Now she was sure she would never have the fluffy guinea pig her father had promised her.

Suddenly the room was filled with strange laughter. . .

Tee hee hee hee!

. . . and the little man stood before her again, singing in his squeaky voice.

The girl told the little man about her father's boasting and the king's order that she should make bank notes out of old fish.

She was just getting to the bit about the melon seeds, when the little man pulled a printing press from his pocket and began throwing the fish in one end and pulling crisp new bank notes from the other, singing as he worked . . .

"Anything, anything," promised the poor girl, frantically searching her apron pockets. But alas! There was nothing there.

The girl gladly agreed and by sunrise not one minnow remained. The room was stacked to the ceiling with neatly folded, slightly smelly bank notes.

"Let's marry immediately!" shouted the king throwing open the door.

Eyebrow jumped up and down with delight. "You see!" he yelled "I told you she was clever. This girl can do ANYTHING! Why I bet . . . I bet . . ."

But the miller's daughter was gone,
down the stairs and out of the palace.

Later, as he walked home, the miller began to feel very sorry about all the porky pies he had been telling, and all the trouble he had caused.

So remembering his promise, he called in at the pet shop and bought his daughter the cutest, fluffiest little guinea pig he could find.

The girl was delighted and soon forgot about the horrid king and the strange little man. But that night as she lay in her bed listening to her new pet running round and round on his squeaky wheel, she heard someone laughing outside her door. . .

The girl didn't wear her apron in bed, so she wept into her pyjamas instead. "Don't take my guinea pig," she pleaded.

The little man felt sorry for her and said. . .

Okay kid. we'll play a game. I'll give you two days to guess my name.

In a flash, he was gone. The girl lay awake
for the rest of the night thinking of likely
names for him.

The next evening, the little man returned.

But the plucky girl was determined to try. "Is it Scrambled Egg Foot?" she asked.

But the little man only laughed. . .

Tee hee hee hee!

. . . and stroked his long orange beard.

"Is it Plum-Plum-Lemon-Moose Carpet Ears?" she asked hopefully.

The little man laughed even more.

"Well then, perhaps it's Hubert Crumpet Trumpet-Bum?" the miller's daughter asked desperately.

The little man screeched with laughter and in a flash, he was gone, leaving the poor girl more miserable than ever.

The old miller didn't like to see his
daughter unhappy, so at breakfast he told
her a story to cheer her up.

"I was delivering flour yesterday when I saw the funniest thing; there was a little man wearing a string vest made of spaghetti, dancing outside a tiny caravan and he was singing the most peculiar song."

"Can you remember the song?" asked the girl, her eyes lighting up.

"Well, yes," said her father. He cleared his throat and sang:

I sing and dance a little jig,
Soon I'll have that guinea pig.
They can weep a bowl of tears.
They won't guess my name
in a billion years.

"It did make me laugh I can tell you!"

"Yes, yes, but didn't he mention HIS NAME?" shouted the girl.

"Whose name, my dear?" asked the puzzled miller.

"THE LITTLE MAN, you old toad!" snapped the girl.

"Oh no," said the miller, "he didn't."

The poor girl began to despair and a big tear ran down her pale cheek and into her boiled egg.

"Don't cry," said her father, "I can tell you his name – it was painted on the side of his caravan: Rumply Crumply Stinky Pin. Magician. (Spaghetti Vests A Speciality)."

"That's it," cried the girl clapping her hands with joy.

That night, as she was feeding her guinea pig, the little man appeared again.

"I'll just try again," said the clever girl. "I might be lucky this time. Is it Benny Badger-Brain or Eddy Earwax-Eater?"

The little man rolled with laughter.

"Perhaps it's Trevor Telephone Bone Helicopter-Head!"

The little man was lying on the bed, kicking his legs in the air.

"I'll have one last try," said the miller's daughter, "and the guinea pig is yours. Is it . . . RUMPLY CRUMPLY STINKY PIN?"

The little man almost choked with rage and vanished in a clap of thunder, filling the air with a strange smell of burning spaghetti and old fish.

So, the miller's daughter lived happily ever after with her guinea pig and her old father, who hardly ever told lies any more.

"What will you call your little pet?"
asked Eyebrow Snailsocks one day. "How
about Guinea-Winnie-Winkie-Wigs or
Pinkie-Poky-Porky-Piggy Pants?"

"Oh no Daddy," said the girl. "I think I'll just call him . . . Fred."

"That is a *very* silly name," said Eyebrow Snailsocks.

And it was.

Moral: A guinea pig is for life, not just for Christmas.